Disney Girls

A Fish Out of Water

Gabrielle Charbonnet

Disney
PRESS

N E W   Y O R K

Printed in the United States of America.

First Edition

3   5   7   9   10   8   6   4   2

The text of this book is set in 15-point Adobe Garamond.

Library of Congress Catalog Card Number: 98-84795

ISBN: 0-7868-4159-1

For more Disney Press fun, visit www.DisneyBooks.com

Contents

Disney Girls

A Fish Out of Water

Chapter One

Rockin' and Rollin'

"Here I go!" I yelled, skating fast. "Watch out!" My Roller Blade wheels zoomed over the smooth pavement. The trick was to go fast, but not *too* fast. I didn't want to lose control. Suddenly the steps appeared before me. I threw out my arms, picked up my feet, and flung myself downward. I flew over the steps. *Wham!* My wheels hit the sidewalk below. I felt myself wobbling, tried to catch my balance, and then the next thing I knew I was sliding on my bottom toward the grass.

When I came to a stop I sat there for a moment, doing

a silent health check. My bottom was sore—I must have hit hard. Everything else was fine. I was glad it was November, so I was wearing long sleeves and jeans. If I'd been in shorts I would have lost serious skin.

"Ariel!" called my best friend, Paula Pinto. "Are you okay?" Holding on to the handrail that divided the steps, she bounced down to me. Her dark eyes showed concern.

I held up my hand. "I'm fine. I was going too fast. Again."

"Work on your angle of approach," Paula advised me.

I grinned at her.

My four other best friends coasted to a stop at the top of the steps. "Ariel, are you okay?" Yukiko Hayashi asked anxiously.

I stood up and brushed off my pants. "I'm fine."

"Well, if you two are done scaring us all half to death, can we take a little break now?" asked Ella O'Connor, crossing her arms over her chest.

"Sure." Paula and I climbed the stairs and we all skated over to our favorite bench. The six of us Disney Girls were in Willow Green, which is a small park in the middle of our Orlando, Florida, suburb of Willow Hill. (I'll explain about the Disney Girls later.)

I sat down gingerly next to Isabelle Beaumont. My friends and I had been skating all morning, and it felt good to rest. I looked around, catching my breath. Paula and I had been working on jumping down three steps on our skates for a couple of weeks now. Paula had managed to do it once. I was still wiping out, but I was getting better.

"Whew," said Jasmine Prentiss, fanning her face. She brushed her long blond hair back over her shoulder. "I'm hot. Did you guys see my famous Prentiss arabesque?"

Isabelle laughed. "Sure did. Very impressive."

"How about the Hayashi maneuver?" asked Yukiko.

I giggled. "It was majorly awesome, Yukiko," I said.

Isabelle and Ella slapped high fives. "Let's hear it for plain old skating," said Isabelle.

"You guys weren't doing plain old skating," I said.

"Well, working on turns and skating backward isn't exactly earth-shattering," said Isabelle comfortably. "But that's okay. I know I'm not a daredevil, like you and Paula."

"And we're not ballerinas, like Jasmine and Yukiko," said Ella. "We're just us. Disney Girls."

"That's good enough for anyone!" I said.

"Speaking of ballerinas," said Jasmine. "Our ballet school is having a special holiday pageant. We're going to do *The Nutcracker*, and everyone in the whole school will have a part."

Jasmine and Yukiko take ballet once a week at Madame Pavlova's Dance Academy.

"Wow," said Paula. "The whole *Nutcracker* ballet?"

"Not the *whole* thing," said Yukiko. "But most of it. Jasmine and I are going to audition for some of the bigger roles."

"That sounds great," said Isabelle.

"It is," said Jasmine excitedly. "It's going to be in the big auditorium at Orlando High. And we're going to have fabulous costumes, and real musicians playing the music. It's a big deal."

My eyes widened. "Too cool," I said, feeling a little envious. "Will you have fancy tutus and ballerina hair-styles and everything?"

"The whole enchilada," said Yukiko, grinning.

Oh, man. Now I was definitely envious. It's not like I'm a ballet freak or anything. In fact, I'm on our local club's swim team, and I love it, love it, love it. (All of my sisters are on the team, too.) But face it: swimming is not that glamorous. The fanciest costumes we get to wear are *bathing suits*. Not even cute bathing suits. Racing suits. I mean, *yawn*. And people don't come to see us looking beautiful and lovely. I'm usually standing there with my hair all sopping wet, or even worse, in a *swim cap*, getting my picture taken for the local newspaper.

So this ballet pageant thing sounded so, so cool. I pictured Jasmine and Yukiko gliding gracefully across a stage as music played . . . I wished I could be part of it, too.

Just as I was about to heave a sigh, Paula jumped up and grabbed her skating helmet. "Okay, guys," she said, buckling the strap. "This time I will conquer the steps." She looked at me. I was already fastening my helmet. "Ready to rock?" she asked.

"Ready to roll," I confirmed, and we left the other four Disney Girls on the bench as we sped off to conquer the steps.

Chapter Two

Totally Death-Defying

Paula and I practiced leaping down the steps about fifty more times before we felt completely ragged out. It's the kind of thing we like to do. Paula and I are *best* best friends. (Just so you'll know, Ella and Yukiko are also *best* best friends, and so are Jasmine and Isabelle.)

Some people are surprised to find out that Paula and I are such tight buds. I guess we do seem pretty different sometimes. Paula is quiet and thoughtful. I'm kind of, well, loud. Paula always sees both sides of an issue. I make snap decisions. It takes a lot to get Paula really mad, and sometimes I seem totally flammable! But then I cool down right away. I like the fact that Paula is pretty even-tempered. If we were both like me, no one could stand it!

But we have a lot in common, too. For example, we're both a little tomboyish. We love to run and jump and climb and skate and swim and bike and dig and build. We both take risks sometimes. We're both brave and strong. I'm so happy the magic brought us together!

I still remember the day we met. I was five, and Paula was six. (Now I'm eight, and she's nine.) My older sisters, Camille and Laurel, were having some kind of all-girl giggle-fest at my house, so I escaped with my bike. Out in our driveway, I set up a ramp, using bricks and some boards. Then I practiced jumping my bike off the ramp. I had just learned how to ride a two-wheeler a couple months before, and my bike was a little big for me. That didn't stop me.

I kept wiping out. I skinned both my knees. Then I noticed a tall, dark-haired girl watching me. She was on her bike, too. I waited for her to say something dumb, like, "Girls don't do things like that." Instead, she rode her bike over. Without saying anything, she coasted to the top of our driveway. She hunkered down over her handlebars, and her eyes narrowed as she stared at the ramp.

She leaped forward on her bike, pedaling hard, standing up to get extra speed. Then she zoomed up the ramp, yanking on her handlebars right as her front wheel left it. Wow! She soared through the air, landed hard, caught herself, and spun in a tight circle to face me. My mouth was hanging open.

I dropped my bike, ran over to her, and put both my hands on her arms. "You're my real sister!" I said. And she grinned.

It turned out that she lived right around the corner from me! I don't know how we hadn't met before. But from that day forward, we were inseparable. (We didn't know it then, but we had *another* huge thing in common. I'll tell you about it in a minute.)

When kindergarten started, I met Ella and Yukiko. They seemed really neat, and we started hanging out. I introduced them to Paula. The four of us just clicked, although we were all pretty different. Like, Ella and Yukiko are much less daring than me or Paula. But they were funny and fun and smart, and we played great games together.

Then one day, we found out what had brought us all together—the one huge thing we all had in common.

Before I reveal what it is, I have to tell you that I am Ariel. I mean, I am really *Ariel,* the Little Mermaid. You just have to accept that.

Before the movie even came out, my sisters and I loved to swim. (Camille is two years older than me, and Laurel is four years older than me. My little sister, Sophie, is two years younger than me.) From the time I could walk, I was very comfortable and happy in the water. I loved swimming pools, the beach, the bathtub, big puddles. I felt at home there.

Then *The Little Mermaid* came out, and it was like, of course! That's me! I mean, we have the same name, we both have long red hair and blue eyes, we're both water creatures, we both like to sing, we both have a bunch of sisters. (Except my father isn't King Triton. He's a pediatrician.) I felt stunned when I saw that movie—as if they had hidden a camera inside my brain and filmed my real life.

But I kept this news to myself. I didn't know what the others would think if I blurted out that I was really supposed to be a mermaid, and not a human. It might sound kind of weird.

Then came that day at Paula's house. Paula, Ella,

Yukiko, and I had gotten together to watch the movie *Pocahontas*. It had just come out on video. We had all seen it in the theater, but I was psyched to see it again.

As we watched the movie, I got a funny feeling. As if I had seen Pocahontas somewhere before. Somewhere in real life. Then Yukiko said, "Oh my gosh." Her eyes were huge, and she turned to stare at Paula. So did Ella. Instantly, I knew what they were thinking. Yukiko said, "Paula, that's you. I see you on the screen, when Pocahontas is there."

I almost fell off my chair. It was true that Paula also has dark hair, dark brown eyes, and light tan skin, like Pocahontas. And she really is Native American, just like Pocahontas. Why hadn't I seen it before?

Paula stopped the movie and looked at us. "It's so weird that you said that," she said. "Because I am Pocahontas. I can't explain it."

Well, after she said that, it was like a huge wave bursting onto the shore. It was totally amazing. Ella said that she had always felt like Cinderella. When I looked at her sandy blond hair and sweet face, I saw it, all at once.

Yukiko said it was obvious that she was Snow White. (Her name means snow in Japanese, and she has *six* little brothers and one baby sister. The Dwarfs!) Even though Yukiko is Japanese-American, it was Snow White's face that I saw when I looked at her.

Paula was Pocahontas, and I was Ariel, the Little Mermaid. We were all Disney princesses, come to life. It was like, *whoa*.

Then last year, Yukiko met Jasmine in her ballet class. Jasmine is Princess Jasmine from *Aladdin*. At first it was hard to see past Jasmine's long blond hair and green eyes, but now it seems totally natural that she looks the way she does.

When school started this year, we found our sixth soul mate. Jasmine's new friend Isabelle turned out to be Belle, from *Beauty and the Beast*. Isabelle is black, with smooth tan skin, dark brown eyes, and lots of little braids all over her head. At first you might not think she seems much like Belle. But as soon as she opens her mouth, it's obvious.

Now the six of us are the Disney Girls—totally best buds. It's magical. It's natural. It's the way it is.

Chapter Three

My Lame Sisters

That evening, the whole time I was setting the table for dinner, I couldn't get the pageant out of my head. I had seen a movie of *The Nutcracker* before, and I remembered the beautiful costumes, the fabulous music, and the incredible ballet dancers leaping across the stage.

As I put forks at each plate, my mind whirred with ideas.

"Okay!" Mom yelled from the kitchen. "Chuck wagon!"

Footsteps pounded all over the house. We live in a pretty big old-fashioned house in Willow Hill. (All the

Disney Girls live in Willow Hill, except for Jasmine. Jasmine's parents are way rich, and they live in a mansion in Wildwood Estates.)

My sisters flew down the back staircase into the kitchen. My dad came in from the study. My dad's parents were from Mexico, and Dad has dark brown hair, brown eyes, and a nice moustache. Mom's family came from Ireland a long time ago, and Mom has bright red hair and blue eyes, like me. All my sisters look like my dad.

When I caught sight of Laurel, I gasped. My mom turned around to see, and she said, "My goodness, Laurie. What's that?"

"It's a *masque*," said Laurel haughtily. (She says a lot of things haughtily. She's twelve.) Her face was covered with a bright green claylike slime. "For my complexion."

"Must you wear it to dinner?" Mom asked.

"Yes," said Laurel. "I must." She took her plate, which Mom had filled, and went into the dining room. I rolled my eyes and grabbed my own plate.

"Extra rice, no string beans, please," I told my mom. She put three string beans on my plate anyway. She's a big believer in vegetables.

Behind me, Sophie picked up her plate. "Extra rice, no string beans, please," she said.

"You love string beans," said Mom in surprise.

"Not anymore," said Sophie. Mom put three on her plate anyway.

I might as well tell you. Sophie idolizes me. Practically from the time she could walk and talk, she's followed me around like a puppy, doing everything I do. Lately it's been getting even worse. If I buy a new T-shirt, she gets one just like it. If I like a new band, she likes them too. Sometimes I think it's pretty funny. Sometimes it's kind of a pain. Mom says she'll grow out of it someday. We'll see.

When we were all sitting down, I told my family about *The Nutcracker* pageant at Madame Pavlova's. "I've been thinking," I said.

"Uh-oh," Camille muttered.

"Always a dangerous thing," Laurel added.

"Maybe we could have some kind of pageant for the swim team," I suggested, ignoring them. "Like a swimming version of some ballet, or even a play." I was into this idea. "After all, they do *Sleeping Beauty* on ice. Why not in the pool?"

"Hmm," my mom said.

"A *swim pageant*?" Laurel shrieked. She stared at me, her fork in midair.

"An underwater ballet?" Camille giggled. "I'm so sure."

Laurel started laughing, and her masque cracked across her face. I folded my arms and glared at her.

"I can just see it," Laurel hooted. "You could wear a rubber swim cap covered with, like, fake flowers. It would be hysterical!"

I stuck my chin out and narrowed my eyes. Across the table, Sophie stuck her chin out and narrowed her eyes.

"It's a *great* idea," Sophie said. "A beautiful water ballet, with fancy costumes and everything."

"Yeah!" I said. At least someone got what I was talking about.

"Yeah," agreed Camille. "Big, fancy costumes. So when you jumped into the water, they would weigh a ton and you'd drown. Not much of a pageant."

"Hush up!" I said angrily.

"Okay, enough," said Mom. "Laurel, Camille, there's no need to be mean. Ariel's idea is a perfectly good one. Synchronized swimming *is* an Olympic sport."

"Yeah!" I said.

"Yeah!" Sophie parrotted.

"Synchra—what?" I asked.

"Synchronized swimming is like ballet in the water," my dad explained. "But there are no big fancy costumes, and the 'dancers' don't tell stories like they do in ballet."

"See, I'm not crazy. Do you think it would work?" I asked eagerly.

"Um," said Dad.

"It *is* an interesting idea," said Mom. "But organizing a pageant would be a huge amount of work. You'd have to pick a play or a ballet, choreograph it with enough parts for everyone, get everyone to practice and learn their parts, organize costumes. All of this would take money, time, and energy. It's an enormous project."

"But Madame Pavlova's is doing it," I pointed out.

"Yeah," said Sophie. "*They're* doing it."

"They're set up to do it," Mom explained. "They do it every year. And performances like that are what ballet is all about. But the swim team has meets and competitions instead. They're just two different things."

"Oh," I said, crestfallen.

"Oh," said Sophie.

I didn't say much for the rest of dinner. I was

disappointed, but I bounced back pretty quickly. My mind started whirring again.

Later on, as I was lying in bed, it suddenly came to me. I was dying to be in a pageant. I wanted to wear beautiful costumes, and have everyone taking pictures of me looking fabulous, instead of like a drowned rat, as usual. Then it hit me: I *could* be in a pageant. I could be in *Madame Pavlova's* pageant. Jasmine and Yukiko had said that everyone who took classes at Madame Pavlova's would have a part in the pageant. So all I had to do was . . . sign up for ballet classes. Bingo!

I congratulated myself for having another brilliant Ariel idea, and ran down the hall to my parents' room.

Chapter Four

When in Doubt, Leap In

"So you see, if I start taking ballet lessons," I explained, "they would give me a part in *The Nutcracker*. Probably not the lead, but another good part. It would be so fantastic!"

"Question," said my dad. "Why aren't you asleep?"

I swatted his leg. "Come on, Dad. This is important. I want to start taking ballet. Mom, can you call Madame Pavlova's tomorrow?"

"Honey, you're already on the swim team," said Mom. "With two or three practices every week. I don't think you have time to take on another commitment."

"I can fit it in," I said confidently. "No problem."

"Also," said Mom, "the other students have been taking ballet since at least September, and many of them have been studying for years, like Jasmine and Yukiko. Ballet isn't as easy as you think it is."

"It can't be as hard as swimming," I argued. "Learning to do a tuck and turn almost gave me a concussion."

Mom and Dad looked at each other.

"I just don't know," said Mom. "Remember when you decided you wanted to take pottery classes?"

"Yeah, so?" I asked.

"Well, they lasted only three weeks," Mom said. "Then there were the photography lessons. We bought you a bunch of expensive equipment, but you quit after two months. And that gymnastics class at the Y—"

"Look, Mom, what's your point?" I interrupted her.

"My point is that you seem happy with the swim team," Mom said patiently. "How long will you stick with this new interest? Why do you want to take ballet?"

"Because I just do," I pleaded. "I've been wanting to for a while. Please, just call Madame Pavlova's tomorrow," I begged. "Call and ask about the beginners' classes. It can't hurt just to try it."

"Well, all right," said Mom. "I'll call and get information. But I'm not making any promises."

"Thanks, Mom!" I jumped up and hugged her. I kissed them both good night, then twirled all the way to my room.

The next day at school, I didn't mention my brilliant plan to my friends. It wasn't certain yet, and I wanted to surprise them. I love surprising them—like the time I came to school with green streaks in my hair. (I thought it would make me look more like a mermaid.) Or the time I decided to eat nothing but seafood for a week—even for breakfast. Or the time I wore two different shoes on a field trip. But that hadn't been on purpose.

At lunchtime, the six of us sat together like we always do. "So the main role, Clara, will be performed by one of the senior students," Jasmine was explaining. "We'll probably get junior chorus roles."

"They'll be more fun, anyway," said Yukiko. "Because we'll do lots of different things. There's a Chinese dance, a Russian dance, an Arabian dance . . . we might get to be in a couple of those. With different costumes."

My eyes lit up. "Cool."

"The littlest parts will just be assigned," said Jasmine.

"For all the beginner students and the little kids."

"I almost wish I was in your ballet school, this sounds like so much fun," Isabelle said with a sigh. "Except I'm such a klutz!"

"If you want, you can help me," Jasmine said. "You can watch my routine and tell me if I make any big mistakes."

"I have an idea," said Ella. "We could rent a video of *The Nutcracker* and maybe you guys could pick up some tips."

"Good thinking," Yukiko said. "Let's try to do that one afternoon this week."

I was getting so excited listening to them talk about it. My parents hadn't given me permission yet, but I was almost sure they would. Just think of how surprised my friends would be when I showed up at ballet class! I could hardly wait. The more I thought about it, the more I was determined to do it.

That afternoon I said good-bye to my friends and leaped off the school bus. Camille stepped off after me. (Ella, Yukiko, Isabelle, Paula, and I all take the school bus. Jasmine's mom usually takes her to school and picks her up.) I raced up our walk and burst through the front door, slamming it behind me.

"I'm home!" I yelled, flinging my backpack onto the chair in the hall.

"No duh," said Laurel, coming out of the kitchen. She was eating a fruit bar. "I bet everyone in the whole neighborhood knows you're home."

I ignored her. "Mom!" I ran into the kitchen and found Mom fixing a snack for Sophie. "Mom! Did you call Madame Pavlova's?"

"Yes," said Mom. "Do you want a glass of milk?"

"Uh-huh. What'd they say?" I sat down at the table and reached for an apple.

"They said at your age, you would be in the older beginner class, which meets on Thursdays. Once a week," Mom said.

"Are you going to take ballet?" asked Sophie.

"I hope so," I said. "Thursdays! That's when Jasmine and Yukiko go. I could carpool with them. We'd go together! Great!" I took a big bite of apple.

"You have swim practice on Thursdays," Mom reminded me. I stopped in mid-chew. Oh, my gosh. Swim practice. I thought of being sopping wet, my fingers and toes all shriveled like prunes. I thought about the smell of chlorine, and how it made my eyes red. "I want to take ballet," I said firmly.

Mom looked shocked. "Honey, you've been swimming since before you could walk. You love swimming."

"I still love swimming," I said. "But I'm ready to try something new. I definitely want to take ballet."

"You can't miss Thursday practice every weekend and stay on the team. That means you'll have to quit the swim team," Mom said doubtfully.

I took a deep breath. "It won't be forever. As soon as they promote me at ballet, I'll go on a different day. Then I can get back on the team. But I know I'll love ballet. I'll love everything about it."

My mom looked at me. "Okay. I'll sign you up for the beginners' class. But *you* have to call Coach Wynoski." Coach Wynoski is my swim coach. I gulped as I thought about explaining it to her. But maybe she would under-stand. The important thing was, I was in! I was going to take ballet. I was going to be in the pageant! I was going to be a real ballerina!

Chapter Five

Presenting Mademoiselle Ariel

Telling Coach Wynoski wasn't too bad. She came over to the house after dinner to talk about it.

"I'm so disappointed that you're quitting the team, Ariel," she said. "You're the best butterflyer in the whole club. We've really come to rely on your skills and your enthusiasm."

Great. Now I felt bad about it.

"Is there some kind of problem with the team?" she asked.

"Oh, no," I said. "I just want to try something new, that's all. I'm sure I'll be back—that is, if there's still a space open." I frowned. I hadn't thought about the possibility that there might *not* be a space open.

Coach Wynoski patted my arm. "For you, Ariel, I'll make sure there's a space open. I just hope you're doing the right thing."

"I am," I said. "There's no reason I can't do both things."

"Okay, then," said Coach. "We'll try to get along without you somehow. Call me as soon as you want to come back. And good luck."

On Wednesday morning, I got dressed and headed downstairs. As I left my room, I saw Sophie duck back into her own room. I shook my head. I knew what was coming.

Get this. When she came down to breakfast five minutes later, she had on the same outfit that I did: red leggings, a white Disney World sweatshirt with Mickey Mouse on it, and sneakers. I sighed. Next thing I knew, she would be dyeing her hair red. I mean, I was flattered and all, but who wants their little sister copying everything they do all the time?

"Guess what?" Sophie said.

"What?" I asked warily, pouring cereal into a bowl.

"I'm going to take ballet, too," Sophie said happily. "I've always liked ballet. I like it better than swimming."

"Mom!" I stared at my mother, who was reading the paper and drinking a cup of coffee. "You let her sign up for ballet?"

My mom looked at me calmly. "They were having a two-for-one special. And Sophie really wanted to."

"But *I'm* taking ballet!" I said.

"I saw no reason Sophie couldn't take it also," Mom said. "Relax. She'll be going on Tuesdays. You won't be in the same class."

I felt disappointed somehow, as if Sophie was horning in on my special thing. Which she was, of course. I guess this meant that Sophie would be in the pageant, too!

I looked at her across the table, and she smiled. She wasn't trying to be mean, or a pain. She just wanted to be *me,* as usual. I groaned to myself and started eating.

On Thursday I could hardly keep my secret. All day, Jasmine and Yukiko talked about going to ballet that afternoon. I couldn't wait to see their faces when I showed up, too!

"You seem awfully hyper today," said Paula after lunch.

"Even more than usual." We were heading over to the tetherball stand in the corner of the school yard. We're both killer tetherball champs. I raised my eyebrows. Paula knows me too well.

"I have a secret," I confided.

"Do you want to tell me?" Paula asked. See? That's what makes Paula so great. Any other friend would have immediately begged me to tell her. But Paula never pushes.

So of course I told her. She was surprised, all right.

"You *love* swimming!" she said. She lowered her voice. "After all, you're a mermaid."

"Half mermaid, half human," I reminded her. "And my human half is dying to take ballet."

"Well, good luck," she said. Why did everyone keep telling me that?

After school, I told my friends that Mom was picking me up to do an errand. I winked at Paula as she got on the school bus. I saw Mrs. Prentiss drive up in her green Jaguar to get Jasmine and Yukiko. Soon I would be carpooling with them!

Mom dropped me off at Madame Pavlova's. The night before, we had gone to Dance World and bought everything I would need for my class. I was disappointed

I wouldn't be wearing beautiful tutus just yet—beginners wore plain black leotards, pale pink tights, and black ballet slippers. But surely I would have a terrific costume for *The Nutcracker*. Something frilly and beautiful. I would look like a fairy godmother.

I jumped out of her car. "Thanks, Mom!" Then I flung open the double glass doors and bounded inside.

Madame Pavlova's assistant, Mademoiselle Sandra, greeted me with a smile. She showed me where the changing room was, and I sped off. I was already wriggling into my leotard when Jasmine and Yukiko came in, chattering. They stopped when they saw me, and their eyes widened.

"Surprise!" I said, throwing out my arms. "Meet your new classmate!"

"You quit the swim team?" Yukiko gasped.

"I'll probably get back on it later," I told her. "For right now, I'm concentrating on ballet. Do you think Madame Pavlova would let me wear a different leotard? I saw some zebra-striped ones at Dance World."

Jasmine shook her head, looking dazed. "Everyone has to look alike, so the teacher can concentrate on the line of your body, instead of the wild pattern of your leotard."

"I just can't believe you're taking ballet," said Yukiko.

I grinned. "I'll keep you on your toes, so to speak."

Jasmine groaned, then smiled. "This is great. The more Disney Girls at Madame Pavlova's, the better. I was trying to get Isabelle to sign up, but she says she's about as graceful as a baby rhino."

"Welcome to ballet," said Yukiko, hugging me. Then it was time for us to split up into our two classes: beginner and intermediate. I raced out of the changing room, psyched to start.

Chapter Six

My Best Friend, Pocahontas

"It was fan*tab*ulous," I told Paula on Friday afternoon. I had headed over to her house after we got home from school. Later, the DGs were meeting at the Cineplex for the 7:30 showing of *The Wizard's Crystal*—some movie that Isabelle had talked all of us into seeing.

In the meantime, I was hanging out at my *best* best friend's house, getting caught up. I hadn't had a chance to fill her in on my ballet class.

"Are there other kids your age in your class?" Paula asked. We were in her backyard, beneath Grandmother Willow. Grandmother Willow is so big and old that her branches hang down to the ground, all around the tree. It makes a secret, circular room. It's a magical place.

"Uh-huh," I said, taking a bite of my Nutlicious bar. Paula was snacking on a small bag of trail mix, but for me, chocolate and peanuts is what blows my hair back. "We're all beginners, but we're seven, eight, and nine years old. I'm the most beginnerish. But you know, I'm already an athlete, so this ballet stuff seems like a snap."

"Really?" asked Paula. "A snap? I thought ballet looked pretty difficult."

"Oh, no," I said, waving my hand. "Piece of cake. There are five basic positions for your feet, and five for your hands. I mean, how difficult is that?"

"There's other stuff, too," Paula said.

I shrugged. "Jumping, leaping, twirling. I do that stuff every day of my life. I'm telling you, I was born for this."

"Gee," said Paula, smiling. "I guess you want to be human, after all."

I laughed. "Wait till you see me in the pageant. They're handing out parts next Tuesday. I can't wait to see my costume. Those black leotards are borrrring."

"I hope you get what you want," said Paula. "You want to play for a while? I'm getting chilly."

We played outside until it got dark, pretending we were members of Pocahontas's tribe. Besides being a mermaid, it's one of my favorite things to do. And it's a special part of being a Disney Girl. We all take turns living each other's secret lives, and it's awesome. Today there was a crisp, autumny feel to the air as we worked in Pocahontas's yard, gathering sticks for a fake campfire, climbing trees to look for white men's ships, playing with Meeko (Paula's *real* pet raccoon), practicing running as fast and as silently as we could.

Finally Damon, Paula's older brother, called her in for dinner, and I ran around the corner to my own house. It was warm and cheerful inside, after the chilly dusk outside. I felt so happy I could sing.

On Saturday morning, I practiced my new ballet moves in my room, in front of my full-length mirror. Mademoiselle Sandra had given me a chart showing the five basic positions, and also some forms for other ballet movements, like *jetés* (jumps), *grands écarts* (splits), and so on. Fortunately, years of swimming had made me strong and limber, and I could do everything easily. Some of my fellow beginners hadn't even been able to do a split!

After a while I realized that Sophie was watching me from the door, copying everything I did. She was looking at me like I was a Nutlicious bar. I sighed. She's only six. And she *is* my only little sister. I could remember when she was just learning to walk and talk. Now she was old enough to watch TV with, and play board games, and even play tetherball sometimes.

"Is that really ballet?" she asked, sounding awed.

"Yep," I said. I made a snap decision. "Do you want to come in and practice with me? You'll be learning all this stuff on Tuesday anyway."

Sophie's brown eyes lit up, and she nodded hard.

So I let her come into my room and stand in front of the mirror with me. I showed her what I was doing, and tried to remember what Mademoiselle Sandra had said while she was teaching it to us. Down the hall, I could hear Laurel and Camille listening to the latest Casey Brothers CD. But I was enjoying teaching Sophie ballet. Even though she was taking ballet just to copy me, I couldn't blame her. It's fun having someone look up to you sometimes. But it would be nice when she grew out of it.

Chapter Seven

My Fabulous Pageant Role

That weekend I begged Yukiko and Jasmine to show me all the ballet stuff they knew. I wanted to be completely prepared for Tuesday, when Madame Pavlova would assign parts in the pageant. On Saturday afternoon I went to Jasmine's house, and on Sunday we met at Yukiko's house because Jasmine's mom was having her garden club over for tea.

I like Yukiko's house. Their dining room table is on the *floor.* I mean, they sit on the floor around a low table. It's cool. Yukiko also has a fountain in her living room. Her stepdad, Mr. Hayashi, designed it. The rest of her house is pretty normal, except that it's full of boys, boys, boys—and her new baby sister, Suzie.

Suzie is awesomely cute and adorable. She's teeny weeny weeny. She has fluffy black hair that sticks straight up, so she always looks kind of surprised. When she gets a little older, Mrs. Hayashi might let us babysit her.

Anyway, at Yukiko's house, we shut ourselves up in Yukiko's room in order to avoid a boy invasion. I mean, her brothers are just wild sometimes. I still jump when I hear things crashing and breaking in the rest of the house, but Yukiko doesn't seem to notice it anymore.

We worked on our ballet for a long time, and I felt like I was getting a handle on it. I could hardly wait for Tuesday.

"Ariel, you've been spacing out all day," Ella said during art class on Tuesday afternoon.

Have I explained about how Orlando Elementary works? The deal is, Ella, Yukiko, and I are all in Ms. Timmons's third-grade class. (We had made a magic wish to be together, and it worked. It always does.)

Paula, Isabelle, and Jasmine are all in Mr. Murchison's fourth-grade class. But for some subjects, like art, music, and gym, our school combines different grades, like third and fourth, or fourth and fifth. It's an excellent system, because it means we six Disney Girls can be together at least once every day, besides lunchtime.

"Sorry," I apologized to Ella now. I continued slathering paint on my easel. Today we were doing free-form painting. "I can't get my mind off the audition today."

"I thought they were assigning roles to beginners," said Isabelle. Her easel was right next to mine. She had tiny flecks of blue paint on her face and hair.

"They are," I explained. "But they'll assign roles based on watching us go through some simple routines. I've been practicing all weekend. I already know what I want my costume to look like."

"Just remember," Jasmine said from behind me. "You don't get to pick it yourself. You just have to take what they give you."

"Oh, I know," I said airily. "But how could it not be terrific?"

I saw Jasmine and Yukiko glance at each other. I wondered if they were worried that I would steal an important part away from them. I knew they didn't have to worry. *The Nutcracker* has a million parts in it—there would be enough to go around.

I looove riding in Mrs. Prentiss's Jaguar. Yukiko, Jasmine, and I were belted into the real leather backseats on the way to Madame Pavlova's. Soft classical music was playing on the car's CD player, getting me into a ballet mood. I pretended Mrs. Prentiss was my chauffeur, and I was a famous ballerina, arriving to perform at a huge theater. All us DGs have biiiig imaginations.

At Madame Pavlova's, we jumped out and thanked Mrs. Prentiss for the ride. Then we ran in and changed as fast as we could. Sophie was there, pulling on her black leotard. Of course, we looked exactly alike, as usual. She smiled at me and gave me a thumbs-up. She hadn't even taken her first lesson yet, but she was officially in the beginner class, so she would have a role in the pageant, just like me. I gave her a quick hug, and hoped she wouldn't be too disappointed with whatever role she got. I knew some people would actually be scenery on stage. Talk about a bummer! Scenery hardly moves at all!

There were three times as many students here today as last Thursday, because everyone was here to try out for parts. I waited around in my boring black leotard, going over my steps in my head.

Groups of students auditioned at the same time. Madame Pavlova would watch them dance across the studio, her eyes dark and calculating. Madame Pavlova is the most glamorous person I know, after Mrs. Prentiss. Madame Pavlova has steel-gray hair that she wears in a bun, usually with a flowing chiffon scarf wrapped around it. She's always graceful, and walks like a real dancer, with her toes pointing outward.

First the major roles were awarded: the best part, for Clara, went to a tall black girl named Bettina. She was a great dancer—even I could tell that. The part of Fritz went to a senior student named Brian. Down the list they went: the Mouse King, Herr Drosselmeyer, the Nutcracker himself, the mother and father, the Sugar Plum Fairy. I was disappointed—I had been hoping that I would be the Sugar Plum Fairy.

Next the intermediate group sashayed, jetéd, twirled, and moved through their routine. I thought Yukiko and Jasmine looked fantastic. Yukiko is one of the tallest girls in her class, and she looked so graceful and willowy. I was really proud of them.

Finally it was time for my group, the beginners, to perform. I threw myself into all my movements, trying to show how strong and quick I was. I finished everything a few steps ahead of everyone else, and I was barely even breathing hard. Then I joined my friends as we waited for our role assignments.

Mademoiselle Sandra consulted with Madame Pavlova. Then she read from a list: "The junior chorus for the Russian dance is . . ." I wondered if I would get a lead chorus part. I hoped Yukiko and Jasmine wouldn't be too upset if I did. It's just that ballet was coming easily to me, like swimming. A lot of things come easily to me. Except reading. And spelling. Spelling is a toughie. Oh, and math! Math is the worst. But science isn't bad, and I love geography. And of course being best buds with Paula has me interested in earth sciences . . .

"Ariel Ramos," said Mademoiselle Sandra.

My head snapped up, and I realized I had been daydreaming through the whole list! I glanced at Jasmine and Yukiko, and they both seemed pleased. I didn't even know what roles they had gotten! And had Mademoiselle

Sandra already said what my role would be? Who was I? What was I? Was I the lead dancer for the Dance of the Snowflakes?

Mademoiselle Sandra smiled at me. "You shall join your friends in the beginner class as a sugarplum," she announced.

A sugarplum? A *sugarplum*? I was going to be a *sugarplum* in Madame Pavlova's holiday pageant. The sugarplums were just one step up from the scenery! Was there some mistake? Had she gotten my name mixed up with someone else's? But Mademoiselle Sandra confirmed it: I was definitely a sugarplum.

I was dumbfounded. But there was nothing to do but make the best of it. So I would be a sugarplum. So what? I bet my costume would be a glorious, plum-colored tutu, with matching toe shoes, and a beautiful headpiece with plum-colored feathers on it . . . I smiled, just thinking about it. This was going to be more than awesome.

Chapter Eight

One Sugarplum Too Many

I'll tell you: it's hard to make the best of a situation when the situation keeps getting worse.

"Get this," I said on Wednesday at lunch. I glumly unwrapped my chicken salad sandwich and let it sit there. "*Sophie* is a sugarplum, too. Can you believe it?"

"Most of the beginners are sugarplums," Jasmine reminded me.

"Yeah, but Sophie is only six years old," I complained. "A *first* grader. Obviously, they lowered their standards for sugarplums after I auditioned."

"Obviously," said Yukiko, trying not to grin.

"It isn't funny," I said grumpily, poking a hole in my sandwich with my finger. "It's bad enough that she always dresses like me, talks like me, and eats like me. Now she's taking over my ballet pageant! It isn't fair."

"Did you talk to your mom about it?" asked Paula.

I nodded. "She said that Sophie had the right to make her own mistakes, just like me. Whatever that means."

"It won't be so bad," Isabelle said. "There will be a whole lot of sugarplums, from what Jasmine told me. You probably won't have to deal with Sophie at all."

"Yeah, maybe so," I said. I took a bite of sandwich.

"I know it's a drag, having her copy you all the time," said Paula. "But she only does it because she thinks you're totally awesome." She grinned at me. "And who could blame her?"

I couldn't help chuckling, and so did my friends. Trust Paula to cheer me up and help me look on the bright side.

"Okay, okay," I said. "Maybe I can stand her being a sugarplum. If I have to."

"Way to go," said Paula.

That afternoon after school I came home and ate a snack. Sophie watched to see what I fixed, then made herself the same thing: a banana and a glass of chocolate milk. I sighed. Sophie has always kind of looked up to me, but lately it had gotten so much worse—it was like she was trying to *be* me. And frankly, I thought one of me was plenty. Why couldn't she try to copy Laurel or Camille? Then I smirked to myself. Let's face it—why would she? Just then my little shadow broke into my thoughts.

"It'll be fun, being sugarplums together, huh?" Sophie asked.

"Oh, sure," I said without enthusiasm.

"We're both Ramoses, and we're both sugarplums in the same pageant," Sophie continued happily. "Maybe people will think we're twins."

I looked at her. I'm at least six inches taller than she is. I have red hair and blue eyes. She has brown hair and brown eyes. Her skin is tanner than mine. We hardly even looked related, much less like twins!

"Sophie," I said impatiently, "there's only one of me, and only one of you. Why aren't you happy just being you?"

Across the table, Sophie's face fell.

"I'm just a little tired of you trying to be me all the time," I muttered. Then I pushed my chair back and hustled out of the kitchen so I wouldn't have to see the hurt look in her eyes.

I went upstairs and flopped on my bed. I didn't want to hurt Sophie's feelings. I didn't want to be mean to her. But she was starting to get on my nerves. I wanted her to quit copying me all the time!

Sighing heavily, I rolled over on my back and looked out my windows. It was getting dark outside earlier and earlier these days. I heard Mom downstairs, starting dinner and calling Laurel to come help her. (We all take turns.) I didn't turn on my lamp, but lay on my bed and watched the last afternoon light filtering through my blue and green stained glass windows. It created pretty patterns on the walls, making it seem as if I was underwater. I've always loved the effect.

All of a sudden I realized I hadn't been swimming in more than a week. So weird—was that the longest I had ever gone without being in the water? I moved my arms through the air, pretending I was doing the crawl, the sidestroke, and my favorite, the butterfly stroke. I thought about how it feels to go gliding through the water, feeling it whoosh past me. It's a magical feeling.

Ever since I can remember, I've always felt most at

home in the water. Mom says even when I was a baby, I cried when she took me out of the bathtub. I'm just really comfortable surrounded by water. Water holds me, supports me, makes me feel like I can do anything. Things that are hard to do on land, like walking on your hands, or doing flips, or backward handsprings, are easy to do in the water.

Now I was taking ballet class—on land. So far ballet didn't seem that *difficult*, but that didn't mean it felt natural. I did feel sort of awkward, doing the ballet movements. But I'd had only one class. As time went on, I was sure I would feel less awkward.

I was sure of it, but I decided a little extra help couldn't hurt. I got out of bed and took my seashell charm from my jewelry box. Each of the Disney Girls has a magic charm that represents her favorite princess. Because I'm Ariel, I have a seashell. Paula has a beautiful silver feather. Yukiko's is a gold heart. Isabelle has a tiny silver mirror. Jasmine wears a small gold lamp. And Ella has a weensy crystal slipper charm. We use our charms to make wishes and to get in touch with the magic in our lives.

Now I held my charm tightly in my hand. I wondered

if I should get a new charm now—of toe shoes, maybe? Anyway. I made my wish:

All the magic powers that be,
Hear me now, my special plea.
It's the mermaid, calling you,
Help me do as humans do.

Then I closed my eyes and imagined myself in my beautiful ballerina costume, curtseying gracefully on a stage. Flashbulbs popped as I blew kisses at the clapping audience. People were throwing red roses at my feet. I was *so* into it.

But as I concentrated, my charm grew warm in my hands and the lovely ballerina image faded. Instead I saw myself the way I always look after a meet: sopping wet, shivering, standing on a box, holding my medal. My hair hung down in long, dark clumps, my eyes were red, and I was trying to smile as people took my picture. Argh! Where was me as a ballerina? I concentrated hard again, but all I saw was myself in a bathing suit. I sighed. Dumb charm. I tossed it back in my jewelry box.

Chapter Nine

Sugarplums Are Tough

From now until the pageant, I would have ballet class twice a week, as Mademoiselle Sandra taught us beginners our choreography. (Choreography means the dance steps.) Senior students were going five days a week, since they had a lot more to learn and memorize. Jasmine and Yukiko were going three times a week, on Monday, Thursday, and Saturday. Jasmine had chorus roles in the Arabian dance and the Chinese dance. Yukiko had three chorus roles, in the Chinese dance, the Russian dance, and the Dance of the Snowflakes. So she would have three different costumes. I was so jealous, but I was happy for them, too. They deserved it.

On Thursday, Mrs. Hayashi gave us a ride to class in their minivan. Little Suzie was strapped in her infant car seat with us in the back, and we took turns trying to make her smile all the way to Madame Pavlova's. I managed to get her to smile twice! She was sooo cute! I wished I remembered when Sophie was that little. She must have been cute once.

Inside, we changed quickly and split up into our groups. There were now two beginner classes (mine and Sophie's) and two intermediate classes all working at the same time. The beginners stayed downstairs in the huge open studio, and the intermediates went upstairs to work in the smaller studios.

Today I was determined to impress Mademoiselle Sandra with my ballet. I had been practicing at home, and had most of it down cold. If she noticed that I was the best in my class, if she saw how terrific I was, maybe it wasn't too late for a role upgrade. Maybe she would even transfer me into the intermediates. I could be with my fellow Disney Girls! That would be *really* magical!

"Welcome, my sugarplums," said Mademoiselle Sandra in her sophisticated French accent. Across the room, I saw Sophie in her leotard starting class with Mademoiselle Bernice, who is another assistant teacher. Sophie looked very serious.

"Today I will begin to teach you your choreography. Along with music, choreography is the most important thing about ballet. Each step must be precisely the same every single time. And you must all move together, as if you were one. You will all be doing the same steps at the exact same time."

I frowned a tiny bit. How would I stand out if we were all doing the exact same thing at the same time? That didn't make sense.

"First I will teach you just a few steps," continued Mademoiselle Sandra. "Then we will put them together. Let's begin."

I decided to stick with what I knew from swimming. So everything that Mademoiselle Sandra showed us how to do, I tried to do better. I did higher jumps, wider splits, bigger movements. And I did it all as fast as I could.

The weird thing was, it didn't impress Mademoiselle

Sandra. I jetéd farther than anyone else, and she said, "A little smaller and more graceful, please."

I whirled in a tight, fast circle, and she said, "A bit slower, Ariel. Softer."

Nothing I did was right. I couldn't understand it. In swimming, I had always worked to be stronger and faster than anyone else. I'm used to slicing through the water, pushing powerfully off the pool wall, diving in headfirst. But in ballet, none of that mattered. In fact, it was bad.

Finally Mademoiselle Sandra seemed to lose her patience. "Ariel, dear," she told me firmly. "Sugarplums do not fling themselves *about*. Sugarplums dance lightly through children's *dreams*. Lightly, like little purple *clouds*."

I sighed and tried to dance more lightly, like a cloud. I have to tell you, being a cloud does not come naturally to me. But I couldn't let it get me down. I had to keep trying. I had worked through problems in swimming before, and I could work through this. If I practiced enough, I knew I could be the star sugarplum, just like I was star of the swim team.

I watched everyone else in the huge wall of mirrors, and tried to match my movements to theirs. It was tough.

They all looked wimpy. They all moved so slowly. I tried to be a softer, gentler Ariel. At least Mademoiselle Sandra quit correcting me all the time. I was getting it. I was improving. I would be a completely fantabulous sugarplum! The music swirled all around me like water.

Chapter Ten

Disney Girl Central

"Pass the salad, please," I asked Ella on Saturday night.

"Does anyone need more soda?" Jasmine offered. We shook our heads. The six of us were seated around Jasmine's kitchen table. It was time for a Disney Girl sleepover! We take turns hosting them every couple of weeks. Here at Jasmine's we were eating lasagna that her housekeeper, Mrs. Perth, made. Later we would go swimming. I couldn't wait!

At my house, we stay up late, sneak downstairs to watch TV, and play practical jokes on my sisters. At Yukiko's house, we order in pizza and eat it at the picnic table in her backyard. Then we spend a lot of time trying to avoid the Dwarfs. Every once in a while, we might actually play with them, like hide-and-seek, and Statue. Paula's house is great for a sleep over, because we get to play with all her pets (she has three dogs, three cats, a raccoon, some fish, and four tiny finches in a cage). At Ella's, we play dress-up. She has more dress-up clothes than anyone I know— all these great sequined gowns and high heels and hats with feathers on them. At Isabelle's house—well, we've had only one sleepover at her house. At first, it was tons of fun. But then Kenny "The Beast" McIlhenny ruined it. He's her next-door neighbor, and he's in her fourth-grade class. He makes us all crazy. Isabelle says she's never, ever having another sleepover. We'll see.

"Everything all right, girls?" asked Mrs. Prentiss, coming into the kitchen. She and Mr. Prentiss were eating in the dining room.

"Fine, thanks, Mrs. Prentiss," we chorused.

"Let us know before you go into the pool," she asked us. "I think Mr. Prentiss is on duty tonight."

"Okay, Mother," said Jasmine.

I was extra-hyped for this sleepover. First, because it would be a fun, relaxing time without me having to think about dancing like a little cloud. Second, because Jasmine's parents had gotten an enclosure for their pool, so now we could swim year-round, instead of just nine months a year. I couldn't wait to plunge into that water.

After dinner, I was ready to leap into my swimsuit.

"Let me see," Jasmine said, tapping a finger against her chin. "Should we watch movies first, or swim first?"

"Swim first!" I yelled.

"Or maybe we should fix some popcorn," suggested Paula.

"No!" I cried. "Don't you want to go swimming?"

"Do you guys want to hear my new Honeygirls CD?" asked Isabelle.

"Swimming, swimming, swimming!" I insisted, my eyes practically popping out of my head. What was wrong with them? Then I realized they were teasing me. One by one, they broke up, laughing and pointing. "Oh, ha, ha," I said, but I was smiling.

"I have an idea," giggled Yukiko. "Maybe we should go swimming."

"Now you're talking," I said, laughing, too.

A minute and a half later, I was up on Jasmine's diving board, poised over the water. It was dark and chilly outside, but inside the enclosure it was comfortable and well-lit. My mouth was almost watering as I waited to slip beneath the smooth surface of the pool.

"Go on," said Paula. "You know you want to."

I dove in. It was fantastic. The warm water flowed around me as if hugging me in welcome. It slid over my skin and made my hair stream out in back of me like a transparent red fin. Ah, heaven. I held my breath effortlessly as I kicked through the water, churning up small, white-capped wavelets. I turned around and around in the water, feeling it holding me up, cradling me. I swam from one end of the pool to the other, turning and splashing and diving and paddling. It seemed like a long time since I had felt so wonderful. I hadn't realized I had missed it so much.

Suddenly a warm wet hand clapped down on my shoulder.

"You're it!" cried Yukiko, and spun away from me. "Polo!"

I grinned and closed my eyes. "Marco!" I called.

"Polo!" I heard five voices say from all over the pool. I started to feel my way around the edge. "Marco!"

* * *

Finally we headed inside and put on our nightgowns. (Mine has a picture of Ariel on it.) We settled down on our sleeping bags in Jasmine's humongous playroom with the wide-screen TV. Jasmine brought up big bowls of ice cream with chocolate sauce. I was starving. We watched *The Incredible Journey*, because Paula wanted to. I love it when the animals talk to each other.

"I have an idea," said Isabelle, when the movie was over. "I brought my mirror. Anyone want to take a look?"

Besides her tiny silver mirror charm, Isabelle also has a magic hand mirror. Sometimes if you look in it, you might see something that could actually come true one day.

The six of us sat in a circle, linked pinkies, and chanted:

"All the magic powers that be,
Hear us now, our special plea.
Of worldly sights please set us free,
And help us see what we should see."

Then Isabelle passed the mirror to Jasmine, and she peered into it. The air was tingling, the way it does when magic is near. Jasmine's nose wrinkled. "Yuck," she said, handing the mirror to Paula. "I saw myself wearing a school uniform from the same boarding school my mom went to."

"That's weird," said Isabelle, as Paula looked deeply into the mirror.

Paula smiled. "I'm wearing a white veterinarian's coat. I'm asking a cat to stick out its tongue and say 'Ah.'"

"I bet that comes true," I said.

Yukiko was next. She smiled, too. "I'm a teenager. I'm taking Suzie shopping at the mall. I'm so glad I have a sister." She handed the mirror to Ella. Ella gazed into it.

"Hey!" she said. "I got a haircut, and I'm wearing different clothes." She passed the mirror to Isabelle.

As Isabelle looked into it, her forehead wrinkled. Suddenly she looked horrified. "Ew!" she cried, thrusting the mirror at me. "Ew! Ew!"

"What was it?" I asked, looking at the mirror. But the image had faded.

"Oh, so gross," moaned Isabelle, covering her face with her hands. "It was me and the Beast—and we were dancing together at our high school prom!"

We all gasped and stared at her. Isabelle and Kenny McIlhenny? A couple? Whoa.

"Remember," said Paula. "Your mirror just shows one possibility. Not what's definitely going to happen."

"Ew," said Isabelle, shuddering.

It was my turn to look into the mirror. The clear image of my face faded, as if someone had fogged the mirror with their breath. I hoped to see myself as a famous ballerina, my hair in braids on top of my head as I pirouetted across a stage.

Nope. What I got was the same image of me, wet, standing on a winner's box, holding up a silver medal and smiling. I sighed and put the mirror down. What did it mean?

Chapter Eleven

The Worst Costume Ever

For the next couple of weeks, I threw myself into ballet. Every Tuesday and Thursday I trotted into Madame Pavlova's, slithered into my leotard, and tried to learn the sugarplum choreography.

Paula had watched me practice at home, and she had tried to help me learn to dance more lightly.

"Have you ever seen a leaf sinking through water?" Paula asked.

"Sure." I stretched up as high as I could, watching myself in the mirror.

"Well, it doesn't drop like a rock," Paula said. "And it doesn't fall straight down. Instead, it twists and bends and very, very slowly sort of *glides* to the bottom."

Paula is so brilliant. All at once I could see a dried tan leaf, gliding in little arcs as it sank to the bottom of a pond. Could I dance like that? I tried.

"I think that's better," said Paula. "I really do."

At class, Mademoiselle Sandra thought I was doing better also. Either that, or she had given me up as hopeless, because she didn't seem to correct me much anymore. Each class, I tried to do my best. Some days went smoothly, and I felt happy and proud. Some days went pretty badly, and I felt discouraged. But it didn't last long.

One night at home I was practicing in the family room, where there was a lot of space. I hummed the music under my breath, counting the steps I had learned.

"One, two, sashay, glide," I murmured. "Then a pivot, and arms go up . . . " I groaned to myself when I saw Sophie watching me from the door. Here we go again, I thought. I braced myself for her to come in and start copying me.

"You forgot the second glide," she said.

I ground to a halt. "What?" I asked Sophie, who was watching me from the door.

"There's a second glide, right after the first," Sophie said. Starting in a corner of the room, humming the same tune, she showed me the dance steps. You know what? She looked great. Maybe she just looked smaller and more like a sugarplum, but she moved easily and gracefully, in a tight little muscled package. She looked better than I did. I sighed.

At our next class, I secretly watched her from across the room, dancing with her group. It wasn't fair! That little pipsqueak knew how to do everything, and do it pretty well! It seemed to come easily to her! Why was I having so much trouble, and she wasn't, and she was just here to copy being *me* in the first place? I almost pulled my hair out.

Twice during those weeks I dreamed that I was swimming. When I woke up, I was disappointed to find myself in my bed.

At last we were only three rehearsals away from the actual pageant. Invitations had been sent: my whole family was coming, and so were the other Disney Girls. I knew everything I had been through up to now would be worth it when they all saw me glide onto the stage in my beautiful, glorious tutu, maybe with flowers woven into my hair. I would pirouette gracefully, up on my toes, and my parents and sisters and friends would all go, "Ahhh . . ."

At the end of the first week of December, the day finally arrived: costume day. It was a Thursday, and Jasmine, Yukiko, and I caught a ride with Mom and Sophie. The four of us hopped out of mom's minivan and ran inside. A tingle of excitement ran down my spine when I saw row after row of beautiful, frilly costumes hanging on wardrobe racks against the wall. One of those would be mine! I was so excited I couldn't stand it.

It was almost impossible for me to concentrate on class that day. Instead of watching my fellow sugarplums to make sure I was keeping in time with them, my eyes kept straying to the rows of costumes. Which one was mine?

By five o'clock, my nerves were stretched to the limit. I would just have to run screaming down the street if Mademoiselle Sandra didn't give me my beautiful costume soon.

"Okay, class, that is it for today," she said, wiping her brow with her little white towel. "I am very pleased with your progress. Now—" She turned to us and smiled. "I shall distribute your costumes. Please remember to take very good care of them—there are no replacements. And remember to bring them with you to the Orlando High auditorium this Saturday for our dress rehearsal."

I was almost quivering with delight and anticipation. At last I would see the costume that would make everything worthwhile. At last I would look and feel like a real ballerina.

Of course Mademoiselle Sandra did not start with me, with *my* costume. Oh, noooo. That would be too easy. Instead I was forced to watch as most of the intermediates got their amazing costumes, made of silk and tulle and ribbons and sparkles and beads and lace and tiny fake flowers that looked like snowflakes. Across the room, Mademoiselle Bernice was handing out costumes to Sophie, Jasmine, and Yukiko. I couldn't wait to rush over there and compare ours.

"And now, for our sugarplums," said Mademoiselle Sandra, consulting her notebook. "Ah, yes. We will begin with Ariel." She smiled at me and reached behind her to the rack. I leaped forward, ready to take my costume. She pulled out a hanger and handed it to me. My heart pounded. It was shiny and plum colored, with a tutu . . . wait. No tutu.

"Um, Mademoiselle?" I asked, examining my hanger. "Is there a part missing? My skirt?"

"No," she said, looking my costume over. "No, my dear, it is all here." She smiled again.

I slanted my head this way and that, trying to figure out what I was seeing on the hanger. It wasn't a tutu. It wasn't a dress, or a tunic. It looked—big. Too big. It looked weird.

"See," said Mademoiselle Sandra. She must have noticed how confused I seemed. "You'll put it on—your arms go here, your legs come out here. Then we stuff the inside with netting, to make it pouf out, so . . ."

It dawned on me. I finally got it. My costume *was* not a lovely, *pretend* version of a sugarplum. My costume was a sugarplum. I would be dressed as a *great, big, round, enormous purple berry*!!! I would look like that girl from *Willie Wonka*! I almost fainted as the horrible truth filtered into my shocked brain.

Not only that, but I was one of the biggest and oldest beginners. Most of my fellow sugarplums were smaller than me. They would be sugarplums, dancing lightly through children's dreams. *I* would be a *humongous* purple *eggplant* galumphing across the stage like some crazed vegetable gone berserk! Now that I saw what I had been working toward all this time, there was only one thing to do.

I burst into tears, ran from the studio, and jumped into my mom's waiting minivan.

Chapter Twelve

I Need All the Magic
I Can Get

"Honey, would you like more mashed potatoes?" Mom asked gently at dinner that night.

I shook my head silently as I scraped up a tiny forkful and put it in my mouth. It tasted like chalk.

"What's for dessert, Mom?" asked Camille. "Do we have any ice cream? Ariel likes that."

"Good idea," said Laurel. "Ariel, would you like some fudge ripple? With a cherry on top?"

I shook my head. I knew I must really look pathetic if

my sisters were being nice to me. Not that they're mean, but we tease each other a lot.

"You're not going to quit ballet, are you?" asked Laurel. "You've been working pretty hard this past month."

"But it would be great to have you back on the team," said Camille quickly. "I've missed you at practice."

"I don't know," I said miserably.

Across the table from me, Sophie was wolfing down her dinner. "I really don't think the costume is that bad," she said, taking a sip of juice. "I think it looks kind of cute. After all, we *are* sugarplums."

"Maybe *you're* a sugarplum," I retorted. "I'm just . . . a fish out of water."

"Well, I'm not going to quit ballet just because you are," said Sophie. She pulled her salad bowl closer and began crunching noisily. "I really like ballet. I like it better than swimming."

"I didn't say I was quitting," I said. "I said I didn't know. May I be excused?"

Mom said I could. I tromped upstairs to my room and threw myself on my bed. It sounds stupid, but I was kind of annoyed that Sophie didn't agree with me. I had been begging her to be herself, and now that she was making up her own mind, I wanted her to be like me! Crazy, huh? I braced my feet up on my wall and thought some more. I didn't like to think of myself as a quitter. On the other hand, I didn't like to think of myself as a horrible, waltzing eggplant, either. I'd be mortified in front of my family and friends.

What was I going to do?

"Ariel, phone!" Mom called. I hadn't even heard it ring.

I went down to Mom's room and threw myself on her bed. Then I picked up the phone. "Hello?"

"Hi," said Jasmine. "I saw you run out of class today—what's wrong?"

I told her.

"Oh. Gee, I thought the sugarplum costumes were cute," said Jasmine. "I saw them last year, and they didn't look too bad."

"Huh," I said, unconvinced.

"What are you going to do?" she asked.

"I don't know. I guess I better go do my homework," I said.

We said good-bye. As soon as I hung up, the phone rang again. It was Yukiko. I had almost the exact same conversation with her.

"You know, I was a sugarplum my first year," said Yukiko. "I liked the costume."

"You were six years old," I reminded her.

"Yes, but I was really tall," she reminded me back. "It'll be fine. You'll see. You'll be surrounded by other sugarplums."

"I'll look like the mother sugarplum, surrounded by her baby plums," I said sourly.

She laughed. We hung up. Guess who called next? Right.

"Hi," I told Paula. "Boy, do I need to talk to you."

"Jasmine told me how upset you are about your costume," said Paula. She always gets right to the point. "What will you do?"

"I don't know," I said. Then I sighed. "I guess I do know. I don't want to be a quitter. And I don't want to look like a spoiled brat, quitting just because I think the costume is awful. I'll do the pageant. But I won't be happy about it."

Paula was quiet for a few moments, the way she is when she's thinking. Then she said, "You know, it sounds like you're majorly concerned with what other people are thinking, instead of what you feel yourself. Like, you hate the costume because you think people will laugh. And you don't want people to think you're a brat. But how do *you* feel? What do *you* want?"

Now I was quiet for a few moments. Sometimes talking with Paula is like having sunshine poured on your brain. "I guess . . . ," I said finally. "I guess what I really wanted was to look fabulous onstage, instead of looking like a bag of wet laundry." It sounded pretty dumb to me, to tell you the truth. "You know, Paula," I said. "I've been a total guppy. I wanted to look good doing something I'm not great at, instead of looking uncool at something I do better than practically anyone else. Not too smart."

Paula chuckled. "It's been a learning experience," she said, imitating her mother's voice. "And you do actually like ballet. So will you be in the pageant?"

"Probably," I said. "I probably will. And thanks."

"What's a Disney Girl for?" said Paula.

After my mom had come in to say good night and make sure I wasn't feeling too bad, I lay on my bed in the darkness. I felt a lot better, but I still cringed when I thought of myself as a huge dancing plum. I needed just a little bit more help.

I crawled out of bed, took my seashell charm from my jewelry box, and climbed back under the covers. I love my seashell charm. It's so pretty and delicate. Dad had given it to me when I was little, when I was sick with laryngitis. I thought about how I had considered trading it in for a ballet charm. I knew I never could.

I held it warmly in my hand and closed my eyes. "Please help me, magic," I whispered. "Help me know what to do."

For once nothing popped into my mind. My charm stayed cool in my hands, as if I had just picked it up out of a stream. I squeezed my eyes shut more tightly and wished harder, but nothing happened. Finally, shaken, I put my charm on my nightstand. Oh, my gosh, I thought miserably. This was going to be a total disaster.

Chapter Thirteen

The Best Sugarplum in the World

"Okay, now we put eyeliner on like this," said Yukiko, leaning over me. "Hold still."

We were backstage at Orlando High School on Sunday afternoon. Our dressing room was full of dancers getting into their costumes. Mademoiselle Sandra was running around with safety pins, hair spray, and spare tights. Mademoiselle Bernice was helping all the littlest kids get into their costumes. Madame Pavlova was conducting a warm-up class for the lead dancers.

Yukiko was wearing a beautiful red silk Chinese vest over a frothy white tutu that stuck straight out. She had a Chinese-looking headpiece pinned to her hair, which was braided on top of her head. She looked so awesome.

Jasmine stood right next to me. They were both helping me get ready. They had each been in pageants before, so they knew what to do. I had to wear makeup! Usually I hate all that paint stuff, but Jasmine explained that we would be dancing under bright lights. If we didn't wear makeup, we would look dead.

I saw Mom helping Sophie get ready across the room. We sugarplums each wore our shiny, poufy costumes. Mademoiselle Sandra had stuffed netting inside so we looked very full and round. Without the netting we looked more like raisins. The best part of our costume was the pretty little headband covered with tiny purple flowers. After the pageant, we would be allowed to keep them!

When I looked at my painted face in the mirror, I could hardly recognize myself. My cheeks were pink, I had black lines around my eyes, and my mouth was very red. I looked just like Yukiko, Jasmine, and the rest of the dancers.

"You'll look great onstage," Jasmine assured me.

She was wearing her first costume, which was a fitted, embroidered Russian vest over a white tutu. She looked beautiful.

I felt almost sick with dread. I always get a little nervous before a big swim meet, but not like this. My palms were sweaty and I wanted to wipe them on my costume. I was breathing hard, and I hadn't even started dancing yet! I tried to remember my dance, but my mind went blank. I pictured myself frozen on stage, unable to move, while the audience pointed at me in pity.

Suddenly, without my even saying anything, Jasmine and Yukiko took my hands and led me behind a little curtain. I felt their pinkies link with mine, and relief flooded through me. I wasn't alone. I had two of my best friends, and I had magic. They would all help me. Very quietly we said:

"All the magic powers that be,
Hear us now, our special plea.
On dancers shine your special light
And help us dance our best tonight."

I felt a little calmer. I smiled at my friends, and we

hugged. Then we heard the opening music begin. The pageant was underway!

Mom and Sophie came over. Sophie looked great. She seemed so proud of her costume, and didn't act nervous at all. We stood together in the wings, watching as the students from Madame Pavlova's performed *The Nutcracker* ballet. We saw dancers rush back to the wings, change costumes, smooth their hair, then swirl out onstage again in a burst of color and music. It was heavenly.

It seemed like only minutes before it was time for the Dance of the Sugarplums. I heard the familiar music begin. When our cue came, Mademoiselle Sandra motioned us to go. I felt shaky and unsure. I swallowed hard. At that moment, I would have given anything to not go on that stage. Next to me, Sophie tucked her hand in mine. It was now or never. I plastered a big smile on my face, squeezed Sophie's hand, and sashayed out onto the stage. Somehow, my feet decided that they knew what to do. I felt the music fill me and lift me up as I glided across the smooth wooden floor. The lights were bright and warm on my face. My arms lifted and my feet moved with quick, precise movements. The audience was a huge dark blur beyond the stage. The music roared in my ears and swirled around me. I matched my steps to Sophie's, copying her perfectly. And suddenly, I was a ballerina. A beautiful, magical ballerina.

Chapter Fourteen

It's a Mermaid's Life For Me

"Oh, and then Jennifer Stone almost tripped over the scenery, and I thought she was going to plow into me, and that we'd all go down like dominoes, and I didn't know what to do, so I just leaped out of the way," said Yukiko breathlessly.

"No one even noticed," Ella said, pushing her sandy blond hair back. "I didn't see anything unusual. I thought you were supposed to do a little jeté there."

We all laughed. The six of us were celebrating a successful pageant at One Scoop Ahead, our favorite ice cream place. Our families took up practically all the other tables. At my family's table, Sophie was already watching the playback of Dad's video camera. He had taped the whole thing. I couldn't wait to see it, but maybe I would save it for the next Disney Girl sleepover.

"Hmm," said Paula, sipping her milk shake. "This is fantastic."

"Mine is good, too," said Ella, licking her raspberry sherbet cone. I had a huge scoop of jamocha fudge almond in front of me, and I was digging in. Being in pageants makes me so hungry.

Jasmine smiled at me. "Are you glad you went through with it?" she asked.

"Yes," I said. "I am. Even though I wish I'd had a different costume, it was still a lot of fun."

"You did a terrific job," said Isabelle. "Considering you've been doing ballet for only a couple of weeks."

"It feels like longer," I said, taking a bite.

"Actually, Ariel," said Yukiko, "you did an awesome job. I wanted to tell you. I've been dancing for years, and I still really have to work at it. But you looked wonderful out there. I bet Madame Pavlova and Mademoiselle Sandra were impressed."

I grinned. "I hope they're not too impressed. I did have a little help, you know."

The six of us smiled at each other, knowing that magic was a part of our lives. It's a great feeling.

"This time next year, we'll be sitting here again," said Yukiko. "And you'll be saying how hard it was to be the lead snowflake in the Dance of the Snowflakes."

I smiled. "They have pretty costumes. But I was hoping for toe shoes, at least."

Jasmine almost choked on a sip of her fruit smoothie. "Toe shoes!" she exclaimed. "People don't get toe shoes till they've taken ballet for years and years!"

"Yeah," said Yukiko. "Your feet have to be pretty toughened up, or else it ruins the bones in your feet."

"It ruins the bones in your feet anyway," said Isabelle. "But it looks so pretty."

We ate our ice cream for a while. I was in pig heaven sitting there. I was with my five best friends, I was nose deep in a scoop of jamocha fudge almond, and the pageant was over. I would never have to be a sugarplum again.

"It won't be long till we start practicing for our spring recital," said Jasmine.

"That'll be fun, Ariel," said Yukiko. "Instead of one big show, we do lots of different little dances. It's great."

"Well, actually . . . ," I said. I had some news for the Disney Girls, but I wasn't sure how to break it to them.

"Just spit it out," Paula advised, reading my mind, as usual.

"I don't think I'll be in the spring recital," I announced.

"What?" Jasmine's green eyes were wide.

"What do you mean?" asked Yukiko. "All of Madame Pavlova's students take part."

I took a deep breath. "I really like ballet," I said. "And I think I could get better and better at it. I like the music, the dancing, and the costumes—even mine. But I've been doing a lot of thinking, and you know what? Even if I did ballet for a hundred years, I wouldn't be as good at it as I am at swimming."

"That's no reason not to do it," Ella said. "You could do it because you enjoy it."

"I know," I said. "But I think the reason I won't ever be fabulous at it is because my heart is somewhere else."

My friends looked at me, then at each other.

"In the water," said Paula. I nodded.

"Yeah. This is one mermaid who tried being a human,

and decided to stay a mermaid. I like ballet, but I loooove swimming. And that's where my heart is."

"You're going back on the team?" asked Isabelle.

"If they have a spot open," I said.

"I'm sure they will," said Paula.

"In the meantime . . . " I said, raising my hand high. My friends all raised their hands to mine in a giant high five.

"It's Disney Girls forever!" we cried.

Here's a sneak preview of

Disney Girls

#5 Cinderella's Castle

I stared at the gingerbread castle I had promised Ms. Timmons and all my friends in third grade. There was only one word for it: DISASTER. The walls lurched crookedly. The roof looked like it was about to cave in. White icing dripped from the edges like library paste. The front door was rough and uneven, as though a rat had gnawed its way in.

I wanted to burst into tears. I had promised to bring a fabulous, fantasy gingerbread Cinderella castle to our school holiday party. Instead I was stuck with something that Frankenstein would feel more at home in.

I had done my best. The other Disney Girls had tried to help me. Even my stepmother and stepsisters had tried to help me. But in the end, it was my failure. I had wanted to look like a hotshot, instead of mousy old Ella O'Connor. But tomorrow I would look like a big nothing.

Unless . . . there was something I hadn't tried yet. Something that had always worked for me before. Something that was my secret—mine and the Disney Girls'.

Right in the middle of the kitchen, I clasped my crystal slipper charm in both hands and closed my eyes. Silently I chanted:

All the magic powers that be,
Hear me now, my special plea.
My royal castle is a mess.
Please make my cake into the best!

Now there was nothing to do but wait.

Read all the books in the *Disney Girls* series!

#1 *One of Us*

Jasmine is thrilled to be a Disney Girl. It means she has four best friends—Ariel, Yukiko, Paula, and Ella. But she still doesn't have a *best,* best friend. Then she meets Isabelle Beaumont, the new girl. Maybe Isabelle could be Jasmine's *best* best friend—but could she be a *Disney Girl*?

#2 *Attack of the Beast: Isabelle's Story*

Isabelle's next-door neighbor Kenny has been a total Beast for as long as she can remember. But now he's gone too far: he secretly videotaped the Disney Girls singing and dancing and acting silly at Isabelle's slumber party. Isabelle vows to get the tape back, but how will she ever get past the Beast?

#3 *And Sleepy Makes Seven*

Mrs. Hayashi is expecting a baby soon, and Yukiko is praying that this time it'll be a girl. She's already got six younger brothers and stepbrothers, and this is her last chance for a sister. All of the Disney Girls are hoping that with a little magic, Yukiko's fondest wish will come true.

#4 *A Fish Out of Water*

Ariel in ballet class? That's like putting a fish in the middle of the desert! Even though Ariel's the star of her swim team, she decides that she wants to spend more time with the other Disney Girls. So she joins Jasmine and Yukiko's ballet class.

But has Ariel made a mistake, or will she trade in her flippers for toe shoes forever?

#5 *Cinderella's Castle*

The Disney Girls are so excited about the school's holiday party. Ella decides that the perfect thing for her to make is an elaborate gingerbread castle. But creating such a complicated confection isn't easy, even for someone as super-organized as Ella. And her stepfamily just doesn't seem to understand how important this is to her. Ella could really use a fairy godmother right now . . .

#6 *One Pet Too Many*

Paula's always loved animals, any animal. Who else would have a pet raccoon, not to mention two cats, a dog, three rabbits, and countless fish? When Paula finds a lost baby armadillo, though, her parents say, "No more pets!"—and that's that. But how much trouble could a baby armadillo be? Plenty, as Paula discovers—especially when she's trying to keep it a secret from her parents.

#7 *Adventure in Walt Disney World:*
A Disney Girls Super Special

The Disney Girls are so excited. They're all going to dress up as their favorite Disney Princesses and participate in the Magic Kingdom Princess Parade. And as a special treat, Jasmine's mom is taking them to stay overnight at a hotel in the park. Magical things are bound to happen to the Disney Girls in the most magical place on earth—and they do . . .